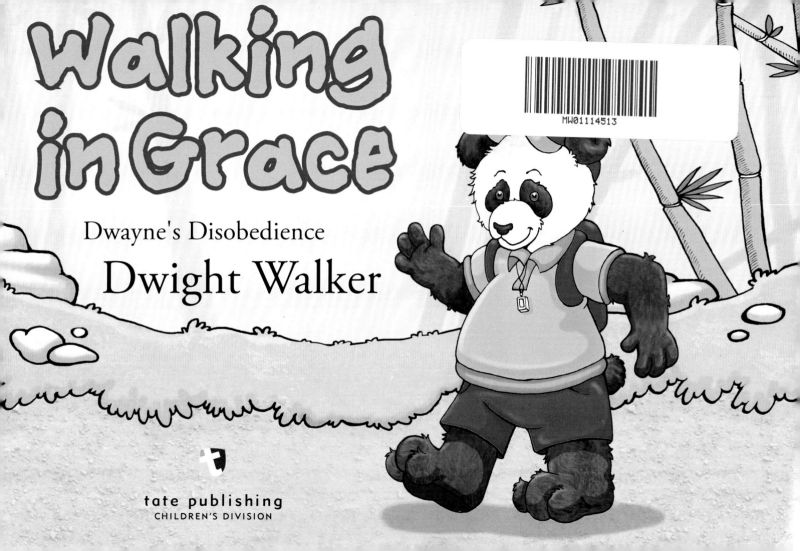

Walking in Grace

Dwayne's Disobedience

Dwight Walker

tate publishing
CHILDREN'S DIVISION

MW01114513

Published by Tate Publishing & Enterprises, LLC
127 E. Trade Center Terrace | Mustang, Oklahoma 73064 USA
1.888.361.9473 | www.tatepublishing.com

Tate Publishing is committed to excellence in the publishing industry. The company reflects the philosophy established by the founders, based on Psalm 68:11,
"The Lord gave the word and great was the company of those who published it."

Book design copyright © 2012 by Tate Publishing, LLC. All rights reserved.
Cover and interior design by Lauro Talibong
Illustrations by Jason Hutton

Published in the United States of America

ISBN: 978-1-62147-182-0
Juvenile Fiction / Religious / Christian / Values & Virtues
Juvenile Fiction / Religious / Christian / Family
12.11.05

Dedication

This book is dedicated to my loving son, Dwight C. Walker, Jr. May the Lord be your captain in your journey to heaven. Always remember to place the Lord at the center of your life and to strive to live your life through his grace and mercy.

Acknowledgments

I would first like to thank the Lord for his continuous grace and mercy over my life. My life is a constant reflection of your wonderful love. Without you, there would be no me.

To my loving wife, Seon Walker, thank you for being a constant support and source of strength to our family. You have played the role of our family's spiritual leader from the beginning. Because of your faith and guidance, I have grown to accept the Lord as my Savior. May the Lord continue to guide you in your walk as we follow your leadership. Finally, to my loving mother: thank you for everything.

Special thanks to: Lacia Johnson, John McCown, Ron Andrews, Shanelle Patterson, Kitson Walker, Saheed Fawehinmi, Darius Lyles, and Corlette Lewis.

"Children, obey your parents in the Lord, for this is right!" (Ephesians 6:1, KJV). Dwayne had just finished saying his prayers, and Mother had asked him to recite his favorite memory verse. Dwayne's mother was a Christian. She read him all the wonderful stories in the Bible, God's special book. Mother also taught Dwayne about Jesus' love and the Ten Commandments. He learned to live like Jesus, and to be obedient and honest at all costs.

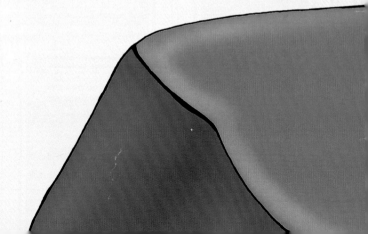

When Dwayne turned seven years old, Mother gave him a golden locket. She said that it was passed down from generations to all the men in her family. The name of Dwayne's great-great grandfather was engraved on it.

The day she gave it to him, Mother said, "You are seven today, the same age my father was when he was given this locket. You should take good care of it. Never let it leave your sight. You should feel very proud to have this locket. You are representing the family when you wear it."

"I promise to take very good care of it, Mother."

And so he did. He treasured the locket and wore it every day, and at night he would place it in a small velvet box by his bed.

One day, Dwayne thought, *I am seven now, and we live just a couple of blocks from school. I am big enough to walk to school by myself.* So he asked his mother.

Mother agreed with Dwayne. However, she expressed one rule. "You can walk to school by yourself, but you must walk the long way."

The long way meant Dwayne had to walk through their neighborhood, around the corner, and past the shops. Dwayne longed to take the shorter way. He wanted to take the trail behind the neighborhood that led to his school. This was the trail all the older kids took.

"Mother?" Dwayne said one Monday morning while he was having his breakfast.

"Yes, son?" Mother replied, smiling as she packed his lunch.

"May I walk through the trail today?" Dwayne's eyes sparkled with delight.

Mother pinched his cheeks playfully. "Now why do you want to take the trail to get to school? What's wrong with the way you always take?"

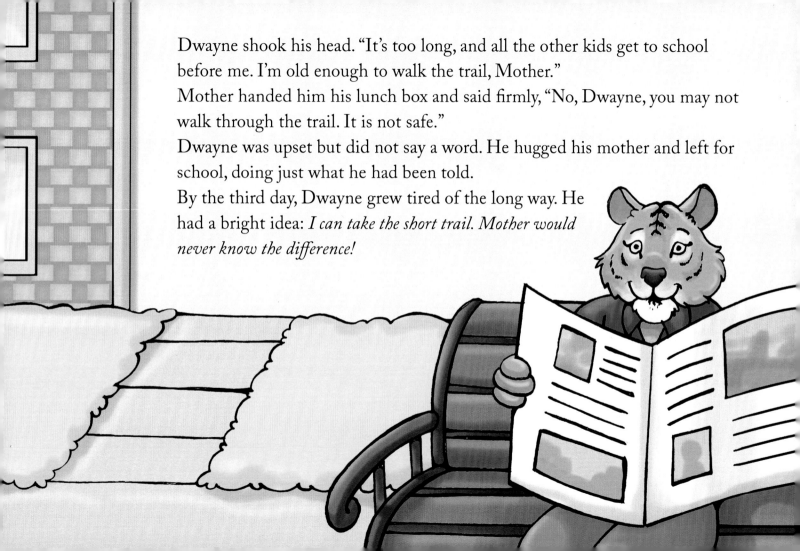

Dwayne shook his head. "It's too long, and all the other kids get to school before me. I'm old enough to walk the trail, Mother."

Mother handed him his lunch box and said firmly, "No, Dwayne, you may not walk through the trail. It is not safe."

Dwayne was upset but did not say a word. He hugged his mother and left for school, doing just what he had been told.

By the third day, Dwayne grew tired of the long way. He had a bright idea: *I can take the short trail. Mother would never know the difference!*

So that very day, Dwayne kissed Mother good-bye and walked toward the trail. He shook with excitement as he walked the trail for the first time. He was even more excited when he saw the older kids who always walked the trail.

I am one of them! Dwayne thought proudly.

All of a sudden, Dwayne felt as if Mother was watching. *Mother is in the house! She cannot see me from here!* Dwayne quickly reminded himself. He continued to walk, reaching school in no time and feeling proud of himself.

A week had passed, and Dwayne had proved Mother wrong. He walked the trail, and nothing bad had happened to him. Plus he got to school faster.

One day, Mother asked, "How has it been walking to school alone?"

"Mother, it has been great! I have been taking the trail, and nothing bad has happened."

Mother grew sad. "I told you not to take the trail." She sat next to him, and put his little hands in hers.

In a serious voice, Mother said, "Dwayne, the long way is the safe way. There are people on the street to look out for you. Mr. Grey the policeman is always there, and the exercise will do you well!"

Dwayne started to frown. "The long way is too long!" he complained.

"That may be true, but the trail is not safe. There are idle boys on that trail who are up to no good. There will be no one to help you if you are in trouble."

By this time, Dwayne had to leave for school, so Mother finished packing his things. She handed him his backpack and said, "Promise me you will take the long way from now on."

Dwayne smiled as he hugged Mother. "Okay, I promise."

Mother hugged him back and said, "Remember Ephesians chapter six verse one." Dwayne knew this Bible verse by heart. "Children, obey your parents in the Lord, for this is right!" he declared, running through the gate.

This made Mother very glad. She closed the gate, hoping that her son would keep those words in his heart and be obedient. That day, Dwayne took the long way to school. He really did want to obey his mother. The next day, he took the long way again. Dwayne took the long way for three whole days. On the fourth day, Dwayne grew tired of the long way and longed to take the trail.

On the fifth day, Dwayne
waved good-bye to Mother and
set out for school. When neither of
them could see the other, he stopped
in his tracks. To his left was the grassy
bank that led to the beginning of the
trail. To his right was the long way through
the neighborhood.

Once again, Dwayne thought, *Mother would never
know if I took the trail or not. All I have to do is slip off the
road.*

Dwayne decided to do just that. He turned left and took the
trail. Just as he began to walk, a gentle but strong voice said,
"Dwayne, my child, do not take the trail."

He looked around him. There was no one there.

Could it be? Dwayne thought. Mother always told Dwayne that Jesus spoke in a still small voice through the Holy Spirit. Dwayne knew Jesus was speaking to him. But he shook his head and kept on walking.

Mom is wrong, and I am right. This trail is safe! Nothing will happen to me.

Dwayne walked halfway along the trail when he saw some older boys. They were not walking to school, and were playing rather rough. The older boys had taken a younger boy's ball. They passed it around to each other, taunting him and refusing to give it back. Dwayne quickly placed his locket in his pocket to hide it.

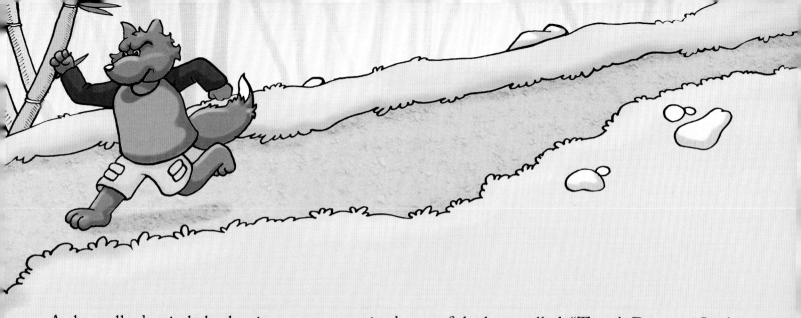

As he walked quietly by, hoping to go unnoticed, one of the boys yelled, "There's Dwayne! Let's get him!"

The boys started to chase Dwayne. He ran as fast as his little feet could take him. He kept running until he reached the end of the trail. He outran the older boys. Ready to celebrate his victory, Dwayne reached for his locket. To his surprise, his pocket was empty! He stood frozen in shock and disbelief that his golden locket was gone.

What have I done? Dwayne asked himself. He began to cry.

Suddenly, he remembered his mother's warning: "Dwayne, the long way is the safe way. The trail is not safe."

Dwayne then cried aloud, "Why did I disobey Mother? Why did I think that she was wrong and I was right?"

As he walked into the schoolyard, Dwayne whispered a little prayer, asking Jesus to forgive him for disobeying his mother.

When Dwayne got home from school, he ran straight to the kitchen where his mother was washing dishes.

"Mother!" Dwayne cried out.

Mother quickly ran to comfort her son. "What's wrong, honey?"

"I disobeyed you. I took the trail again today. The older boys chased me, and I lost my locket. I'm sorry. I'll never disobey you again."

Mother was upset, but as she looked at her son, she saw how sorry he was. She also remembered that Jesus, in his love, forgives when we do wrong.

She comforted Dwayne, hugging him and letting him know that she forgave him. Then she whispered in his ear, "Son, I see that you have learned your lesson, but there is a price to pay for disobeying me. You have lost the locket."

"I'm so sorry, Mother!" Dwayne buried his face in her chest, tears rolling down his cheeks.

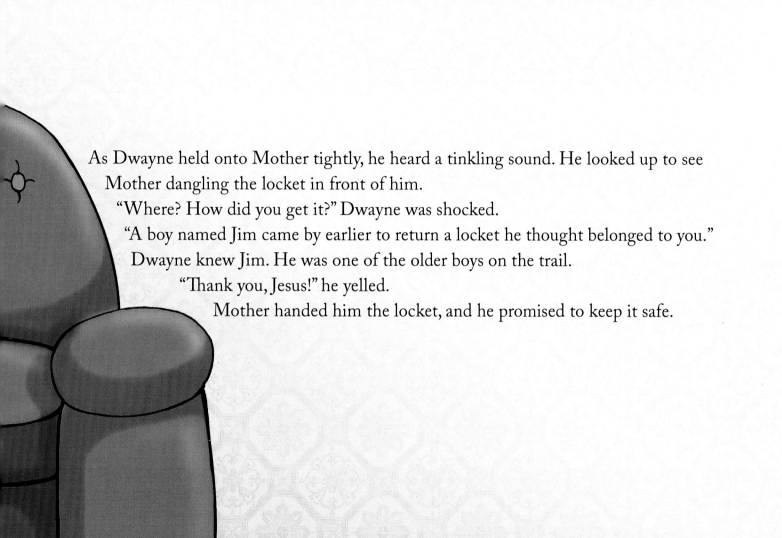

As Dwayne held onto Mother tightly, he heard a tinkling sound. He looked up to see Mother dangling the locket in front of him.

"Where? How did you get it?" Dwayne was shocked.

"A boy named Jim came by earlier to return a locket he thought belonged to you."

Dwayne knew Jim. He was one of the older boys on the trail.

"Thank you, Jesus!" he yelled.

Mother handed him the locket, and he promised to keep it safe.

e|LIVE

listen|imagine|view|experience

AUDIO BOOK DOWNLOAD INCLUDED WITH THIS BOOK!

In your hands you hold a complete digital entertainment package. In addition to the paper version, you receive a free download of the audio version of this book. Simply use the code listed below when visiting our website. Once downloaded to your computer, you can listen to the book through your computerís speakers, burn it to an audio CD or save the file to your portable music device (such as Appleís popular iPod) and listen on the go!

How to get your free audio book digital download:

1. Visit www.tatepublishing.com and click on the e|LIVE logo on the home page.
2. Enter the following coupon code:
   7186-ef9c-30b4-7e7a-143d-0e94-09e8-20b1
3. Download the audio book from your e|LIVE digital locker and begin enjoying your new digital entertainment package today!